T0368450

THE FURTHER ADVENTURES OF 3 BEST FRIENDS

"ADVENTURE IN THE BIG CITY"

STORY & ILLUSTRATIONS

BY

ACKNOWLEDGEMENTS:
To Cecile Paquette
   for her suggestions and corrections
Anna Gagne
   for her suggestions and encouragements

DEACON GABE GAGNÉ

Book 2

THE ADVENTURS OF THREE BEST FRIENDS   BOOK 2

What a celebration there was on the Island for the two boys! Everyone was praising them and especially Suzie Wilson and her parents.

Then things quieted down and returned to normal but it would never be REALLY normal again.

Within two weeks the boys were called to the airport on the mainland. It was the FAA(Federal Aviation Administration). An official looking middle-aged man had summoned the boys.

He first congratulated them for their exploit!
Then he told them that they were obliged to get their pilot's license if they wanted to fly their experimental plane again. Not only that but their plane would have to be inspected and registered.

He told them because it had been an emergency that there would be no fine. He shook their hands and departed.

After the boys had thanked the FAA official they returned to the Island and turned to the next project: "souping up" Johnny's wheelchair!

The very first thing they had to do was to visit the library to research what the speed of the wheelchair would have to be. They had to explain to the librarian what they meant by "souping it up" and that is, their intention was to install an electric motor that would enable speeding it up.

They wanted to know, first, what the running speed was for the average man.

They found out that that speed was a about 6 mph.

So, it was decided the wheelchair would have to have a top speed of as close to 10 mph as possible! And in total safety of course!

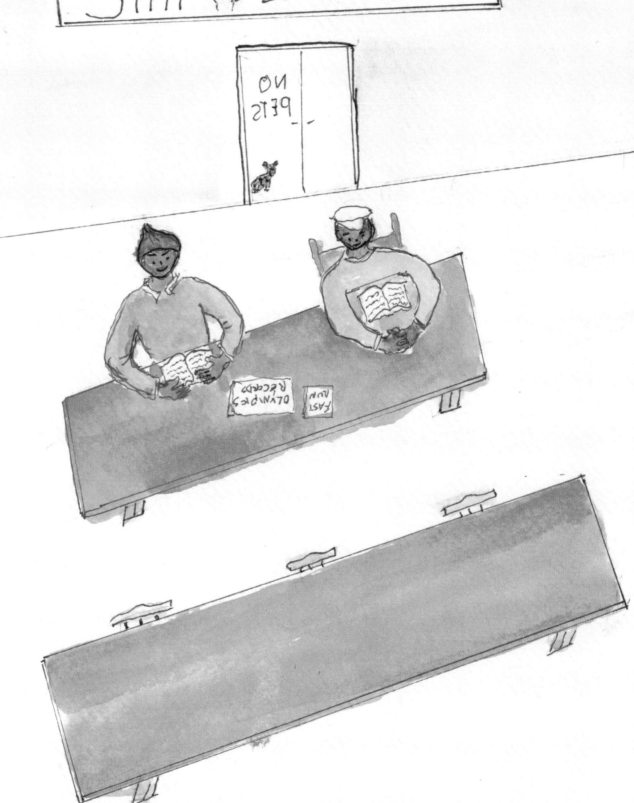

But in order to see their project go from paper to reality it was necessary to find funding for the project.

The boys devised a plan to submit some of their ideas to corporations which, hopefully, would give them a reward for their suggestions.

So, they spent their free time coming up with some ideas for the APPLE® iPhone® and Elon Musk for his vehicles!

SUCCESS! The Apple® company paid them $1000 for their suggestion to install photo voltaic cells on the face of their iPhones (these would charge the phone when they are used in lighted areas).

Elon Musk was still thinking.

So, they started working on "souping up" Johnny's wheelchair. At first they weren't completely successful. But eventually and rather quickly they came up with a working model!

SUBMITED TO APPLE ®

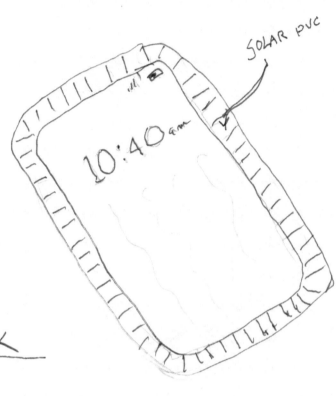

SOLAR PVC

10:40 am

ELONMUSK

FACIAL RECOGNITION CAMERA

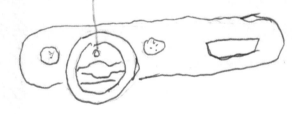

THUMBPRINT READER

AUTO THEFT PREVENTION

It was the first Saturday of summer vacation. They boarded the ferry and made their way to the Big City.

Unfortunately, they had to leave their cat Toby at home. This would prove to be the best for Toby as you will soon see!

Once in the city they strolled along the wide grand Avenue.

It would soon be lunch time and the boys started looking for a diner.

Suddenly they heard a commotion not too far away! Seemingly from nowhere came a guy who was in an awful hurry.

He was wearing a hoodie and carrying a little dog. From around the corner, they heard an alarmed cry for help: "Stop that man, he's got my dog" a lady cried!

The hooded man with the dog narrowly missed falling over Johnny's wheel chair!

It didn't take long for Johnny to figure things out.
He said to Billy: "I'm going after him!" Billy said: "Quick Johnny get the dog back, GO!"

Johnny pushes the joy stick forward and the wheel chair comes alive!

He is in full pursuit!

Billy was watching the race very closely and hoped their newest innovation would not disappoint them.
But mostly he wanted to return the little dog to its owner!

As far as he could see Johnny was gaining on the dog napper!

And when Johnny is close enough, he takes hold of the BOLA WRAP® he had brought just in case.

Holding it tightly he took only a second to aim it at the thief's knees and fires it off!

The bola wraps itself around his knees and the thief falls flat on his stomach and at the same time liberating the little dog.

The little pooch was only too glad to jump onto Johnny's lap because Johnny was calling it ever so gently!

The boys made their way around the corner from where the cry for help came. All the while Johnny was able to successfully comfort the little dog.

There they saw an elderly lady, clearly upset, and a young girl doing her best to comfort her.

As the boys made their way closer to them, they recognized their classmate Suzzie!

As soon as elderly lady saw her beloved dog, her tears turned from sorrow to joy!

Suzzie Helped her elderly friend make her way towards the boy on the wheelchair who was cuddling her beloved pet!

After the reunion of the grateful elderly lady with her pet dog Suzie did the introductions. It turned out that the elderly lady was actually Suzie's grandmother who lived in the big city!

Suzie introduced her as Molly. She was fond of calling her Gramm. When Gramm found out the two boys were responsible for saving her granddaughter, she looked intently at them and expressed her heartfelt thanks for all the boys had done for them.

The boys were embarrassed by the expressions of gratitude and Gramm insisted on inviting them to have lunch with her and Suzie.

In no time they were finishing their meal and Gramm asked them "Boys my friend had her car stolen the other day. I sure would like someone to find some way of stopping those hoodlums COLD! Could YOU do it?"

DINER

The boys said they would be more than happy to tackle that problem but added that their funds were really low and they were eagerly waiting for Elon Musk to answer their suggestions.

When Suzie heard this, she said to Gramm " Gramm maybe you could help the boys with funds while they wait for Elon Musk's reply."

Gramm immediately said: "Why of course! You boys have helped us so much already, I'll be glad to bankroll you. You've already earned it!"

And so, it was agreed. The boys would start working on a theft deterrent for cars as soon as they returned to the Island.

When the mechanism was ready, they would need to have the car at their shop so that they could install it.

At the end of the day they said their goodbyes and the boys took the last ferry back to the island, but they weren't alone! Suzie was with them!

Deep inside they all knew that all three of them were friends and would always be a team!

The END
of
THIS
ADVENTURE

LOOK FOR

THE NEXT ONE

AuthorHouse™
1663 Liberty Drive
Bloomington, IN 47403
www.authorhouse.com
Phone: 833-262-8899

This book is printed on acid-free paper.

ISBN: 979-8-8230-3746-4 (sc)
ISBN: 979-8-8230-3747-1 (e)

Library of Congress Control Number: 2024921219

Print information available on the last page.

Published by AuthorHouse 11/07/2024

authorHOUSE